BETRAYAL!

Brian, who was walking across the camp with Dave, Slick, and Lucius, spotted Will and eagerly extended his hand for a low five.

"Too bad you got stuck with the Tar Heels," Brian told Will.

"It's no big deal," Will replied. "This whole place is awesome! Our coach really knows his hoops, and we've learned a ton of new stuff already."

"Who is this guy?" Slick asked. "Some teacher's pet?"

"Teacher's pet?" Brian replied. "Back in Branford, Will usually thinks he's the *teacher*!"

Slick and Lucius laughed. Will shot Brian a look, as if to ask, "Hey, whose side are you on?"

Brian immediately regretted his wisecrack. But the joke had just slipped out . . . and he wasn't about to take it back.

Don't miss any of the books in

—a slammin', jammin', in-your-face action series,
new from Bantam Books!

#1 Crashing the Boards

#2 In Your Face!

#3 Trash Talk

#4 Monster Jam

Coming soon:
#5 One on One

MONSTER JAM

by
Hank Herman

BANTAM BOOKS
NEW YORK · TORONTO · LONDON · SYDNEY · AUCKLAND

RL 2.6, 007-010

MONSTER JAM
A Bantam Book / April 1996

Produced by Daniel Weiss Associates, Inc.
33 West 17th Street
New York, NY 10011

Cover art by Jeff Mangiat

ISBN: 0-553-48276-9
Published simultaneously in the United States and Canada

*Bantam Books are published by Bantam Books, a division of Bantam
Doubleday Dell Publishing Group, Inc. Its trademark, consisting of the
words "Bantam Books" and the portrayal of a rooster, is Registered in U.S.
Patent and Trademark Office and in other countries. Marca Registrada.
Bantam Books, 1540 Broadway, New York, New York 10036.*

PRINTED IN THE UNITED STATES OF AMERICA

OPM   0 9 8 7 6 5 4 3 2 1

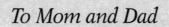

To Mom and Dad

"Brian Simmons, Wolverines."

Brian jumped high in the air, pumped his fist, and cried, "Yes!" Then he ran happily to the other end of the gym, where the Wolverines were lining up. David Danzig, his hometown buddy, greeted him with a low five.

"Show time!" they shouted together.

Brian and Dave were not only next-door neighbors back home in Branford, they were also teammates on the Branford Bulls, a basketball team that played against other squads of ten- and eleven-year-olds. Since the Bulls played only on weekends, Brian and Dave were able to come to the exclusive All-Star Hoops Camp on Lake Winnetoba without even missing a game. Will Hopwood, another member of the Bulls, had also come along, but he was still waiting for his name to be called.

Brian had told his parents that he was excited about learning new basketball techniques and making new friends. But secretly he hoped that all three of the inseparable Bulls—himself, Dave, and Will—would be together all week at camp. So far, so good.

Rock Thomas, the camp director, continued the roll call. Rock was a huge African American man with a shaved head and muscles that looked as if they were made out of, well, rock. Brian *never* wanted to end up on Rock's bad side. His voice was so powerful it sounded as though he were speaking through a bullhorn.

"Otto Meyerson," Rock called. "Runnin' Rebels!"

Brian stiffened. "*Otto's* here?" he asked Dave. "Can't we get away from that loser for a *week?*"

Otto Meyerson was the ringleader of the Sampton Slashers, the Bulls' arch-rivals. The Slashers somehow managed to find the most talented yet most obnoxious players around.

"Hey, man," Dave consoled Brian. "Otto's over there with the Runnin' Rebels, and we're here with the Wolverines. At least we don't have to share a cabin with him. Could you imagine coming all the way out to Lake Winnetoba and having Otto Meyerson as your bunk mate?"

"You're right—it could be worse," Brian agreed. "And maybe we won't have to see his ugly freckled face until the Monster Jam tournament on Friday."

Rock continued to boom out the names. "Charlie Evans, Tar Heels. Anthony DePascual, Blue Devils. Ryan Allen, Hoosiers . . ."

Brian's gaze took in the gleaming floor, the huge electronic scoreboard, and the extraordinarily high ceiling of the vast gym they were in. "Man, would you look at this place," he whispered to Dave. "It's like an NBA arena! What were the other Bulls *thinking* when they decided not to come? Like hanging out listening to Mr. Bowman talk is really going to compare to this!" Mr. Bowman was Nate's father. Nate was one of the Bulls' two teenage coaches. All the Bulls enjoyed listening to Mr. Bowman's advice about basketball—and life in general. But was that more fun than a week of intense hoops at a dream camp like *this*?

"Well," Dave began, "Derek and Jo probably figured they're going to be all-stars in our league anyway. But Mark? And Chunky?" He laughed, tossing his long blond hair out of his eyes. "Those two ought to be first in line here, begging to get their game together!"

"Reggie Saunders, Wildcats." Rock continued reading out the team assignments. "Matt Leonard, Hoyas. Will Hopwood . . ."

"Okay, here it comes. Listen!" Brian whispered, excited.

". . . Tar Heels."

"Man, I knew it!" Brian shouted, stomping his foot with disappointment. "If only Will had been on the Wolverines. We would have ruled!"

A very tall, very pale man about twenty years old had overheard Brian's complaint. "Can't have more than two guys from the same town on a team," he said. Brian figured he must be the Wolverines' counselor.

"Why's that?" Brian asked.

"Rock likes it that way," the counselor answered. "He says it encourages you guys to make new friends. Also makes you think more about basketball than about goofing off with your buddies."

Brian studied the counselor while he

spoke. He was six-five, at least. He wore his basketball shorts super tight, the way the NBA guys used to in the old days. He also had his white socks pulled way up high. On his face were heavy black-rimmed glasses. *Let's hope this guy can play,* Brian thought, *because he sure looks like a geek.*

"L. T. Burns, Bruins." Rock kept the names coming. "Slick Washington, Wolverines."

Brian watched while the latest Wolverine strutted across the gym as if he had all the time in the world. Slick was a tall kid whose black skin was a few shades darker than Brian's own. He wore his hair cropped real close to his scalp, so that from a distance it almost looked as if his head were shaved. His shorts were so baggy they made Dave's look snug—and Dave was known as Droopy back home because he wore the longest, loosest shorts in Branford.

When the new player reached the Wolverines, he extended his hand to a shorter black kid named Lucius Lanier.

6

They touched fists: first Slick on top, then Lucius, then both in the middle. *Buddies from home, obviously,* Brian gathered.

He also noticed a gold chain the newcomer wore around his neck, with *Slick* lettered in script. Most impressive, though, was the dazzling smile on Slick's face. It reminded Brian of Magic Johnson's.

Slick was the eighth and final player to be named to the Wolverines. Their counselor sat them all down under the basket nearest the entrance to the gym.

Finally, Brian thought. *Time to play ball.*

CHAPTER
2

"Gentlemen," the Wolverines' counselor began. His voice, Brian noticed, was surprisingly high for a man his size. "Welcome to All-Star Hoops Camp. I'm Lew Waller, your coach and your counselor. I play basketball for DePaul University. If you want, you can call me Big Lew."

"Big *Loser* would be more like it," Slick cracked under his breath. "If he plays for DePaul, then my mother plays for UCLA!"

Lucius laughed at the put-down. Brian and Dave looked at each other and chuckled nervously.

"The first Wolverines' rule," Big Lew continued, "has just been broken by Mr. Washington. Nobody talks while the coach is talking. Mr. Washington, would you please take two laps around the gym for me?"

"For you, anything," Slick replied sarcastically through his Magic-like grin. He got himself up very deliberately and set out on the slowest two laps Brian had ever seen.

"Actually," Big Lew went on, "what I just gave Washington wasn't much of a punishment. You guys are all going to do a heck of a lot more running than that before the week is out. Because what my team is about is sweat, desire, teamwork, and defense, defense, defense!"

Brian noticed Lucius Lanier roll his eyes. "Sounds like a barrel of laughs," Lucius muttered, so that only the kids could hear.

"First," Big Lew said, "let's run over to the baseline and get ready for some suicides. That's the way we'll be starting every practice."

Slick, who had just returned from his second lap, said, "Yo, Big Lew, is this *basketball* camp or *boot* camp?"

All the Wolverines laughed.

"Call it whatever you want, Mr. Washington," Big Lew replied evenly. "Just stick with me and you'll be kicking everyone's butt by Friday."

"We can kick everyone's butt right now," Slick responded. "Right, Lucius?"

His sidekick nodded automatically. Brian wasn't sure what to make of this pair. They might be troublemakers, but they sure were entertaining!

"Okay, line up," Big Lew called. The Wolverines took their places along the baseline. "One, two, three . . . go!"

Six of the eight players hustled as if their lives depended on it. They ran to the foul line, slapped the floor, then ran back to the baseline. They ran to the center stripe, touched the court, and then ran back to the baseline. They ran to the opposing foul line, bent and touched, then ran back to the baseline. Finally they ran baseline to baseline.

Big Lew had them do this drill six times without a break. All the time, he encouraged them: "Come on, guys, you can do it! Let's go, Wolverines, faster! Touch the floor every time!"

While the rest of the Wolverines responded to Big Lew's cheerleading, Slick and Lucius just went through the motions. Brian realized they were allowing themselves to be lapped so that they wouldn't have to do all six suicides. He wondered if Big Lew would pick up on their trick.

"All right, gentlemen," Big Lew called out, "now two lines for layups. And let's put a little hustle into this, you two," he said, eyeing Slick and Lucius.

I guess he noticed, all right, Brian thought.

Brian knew the layup drill served a lot of purposes. It worked as a warm-up, and it was good shooting practice.

But it was also a convenient way for a coach to quickly tell who could play and who really needed help.

Brian dribbled in from the right side at a forty-five-degree angle from the basket, his eyes fixed on the rim. He went up with his right leg bent and right arm extended, as if they were both on a string, and gently laid the ball in off the glass. Perfect form—he could feel it.

Brian saw that Dave couldn't resist dribbling behind his back when he got his hands on the ball. It was almost automatic for him. But he made his layup in a no-nonsense way.

Next it was Slick Washington's turn. He went high in the air, released the ball, then slapped the bottom of the backboard with his shooting hand. The hot-dogging threw his shot off ever so slightly. The ball rolled around the rim and dropped out.

"This is a layup drill, not a slam-dunk

contest," Big Lew shouted. "No points for style. Just make your layups!"

After all the players had taken half a dozen layups from the right side and half a dozen from the left, Big Lew blew his whistle. "Okay, gentlemen," he called, "I'm sure you all know, or at least you *think* you know, a lot about offense. What we're going to focus on today is defense. Because defense is what wins ball games."

Big Lew then demonstrated the proper defensive stance: crouched low, legs apart, one hand held high, one hand low. He showed how to slide forward, backward, left, and right—without ever crossing his feet.

Brian had practiced this crabwalk before with Jim and Nate, the Branford Bulls' coaches. But never for this long! Big Lew corrected every misstep, every wrong hand position. And if a player didn't move quickly enough, the counselor made him do the whole routine over again. Brian knew he'd hear the sound of screeching sneakers in his dreams that night!

SCREECH!

Big Lew had said they'd work on the crab-walk drill for five minutes, but Brian could have sworn they'd been at it for thirty—at least. His thighs were throbbing when he finally saw the counselor put the whistle to his lips.

"Next on the agenda—" Big Lew began.

"Do you think whatever's next on the agenda might possibly involve the use of a basketball?" Slick interrupted with exaggerated politeness.

"As a matter of fact, Mr. Washington, it just so happens it *does*." At that moment the counselor unexpectedly threw a hard two-hand pass to Slick. Slick was caught off guard, and the ball hit him squarely in the chest.

"Today," Big Lew went on, "you men are going to learn the most fundamental pass in basketball: the two-hand chest pass, just as I demonstrated to Mr. Washington over here. Let's make two lines. You three guys here with Washington, the rest of you over there with Simmons."

Slick Washington went first. He drew the ball in toward his chest with two hands. As he stepped forward with his left foot, he propelled the ball like an arrow to Brian, who didn't even have to move his hands to catch it.

"Perfect," Big Lew said to Slick. "You're a quick learner."

The ball zipped up and back down the line. Most of the passes were on the money.

When the ball had made its way back up the line to Slick, he caught it with one hand. Then he directed it back to Brian with that same hand, without really catching it. Brian had seen guys do that all the time on TV.

"*Two* hands, Mr. Washington," Big Lew yelled.

"I got it to him perfectly with one hand, didn't I? What's wrong with that?" Slick asked.

"No one on the Wolverines is going to be throwing no-look passes or behind-the-back passes, and no one is going to be passing off the dribble. This isn't the NBA. We're going to stick to fundamentals. You got away with it this time, but in a game you might not be so lucky."

"Did I hear the word *game*, man?" Slick asked. "Now *that's* sounding all right!" He winked in the direction of his teammates. "If you ask me, I think it's time for a scrimmage."

"I don't remember asking you, Washington," Big Lew replied. "Anyway, there'll be plenty of time for scrimmaging over the next few days." He pounded the ball on the floor loudly a few times for emphasis. "Okay, guys— back to basics!" The counselor turned and walked away from the group in his very distinctive pigeon-toed gait.

Slick stepped forward and walked between the two lines, pigeon-toed. "Okay, guys, back to basics," he mimicked in a high-pitched voice. His imitation of Big Lew was dead on. Brian didn't want to get in trouble, but he couldn't help laughing.

When the practice session was over, the

Wolverines filed out of the gym. They followed a blacktop path to the white clapboard cafeteria at the top of the hill. The Tar Heels were on their way down the same path, having just finished lunch.

Brian, who was walking with Dave, Slick, and Lucius, spotted Will and eagerly extended his hand for a low five.

"Too bad you got stuck with the Tar Heels," Brian told Will. "Dave and I were kind of hoping you'd wind up on the Wolverines with us." With a laugh, he added, "Maybe we can pick you up for a future draft choice."

"It would've been cool, but it's no big deal," Will replied. Will was tall, even taller than Slick. He had short dark hair, dark eyes, and *huge* hands—perfect for basketball. "Hey," Will continued, "this whole place is awesome! The gym is *humongous,* and our coach really knows his hoops. We've learned a ton of new stuff already."

Slick screwed up his face, as if he couldn't believe what he was hearing. "Who is this guy, some teacher's pet?"

he asked, winking at Dave and Brian.

"Teacher's pet?" Brian replied. "Are you kidding? Back in Branford, Will usually thinks he's the *teacher*!"

Slick and Lucius laughed, as did the rest of the Wolverines. Will shot Brian a look, as if to say, "Hey, whose side are you on?"

Brian immediately regretted his wisecrack. But the joke had just slipped out . . . and he wasn't about to take it back.

CHAPTER 3

"Okay, Wolverines, lights out. No more talking," Big Lew called across the cabin.

Brian snuggled into his sleeping bag as Big Lew snapped off the lights. He kind of wished the porch light had been left on. It seemed really *dark*.

Brian thought about how his mom always tucked him in at night. And how reassuring he found it to hear the even breathing of the twins, Todd and Ali, from their rooms.

"Hey, Dave, you still awake?" he asked in a low voice.

"No, Brian," Dave hissed back. "I fell

asleep the moment Big Lew shut the light off. *Of course* I'm still awake."

"Just checking," Brian whispered. He paused. "Man, is this camp *sweet,* or what?" he asked. "I never thought we'd be playing in a gym like this! And getting on the same team. What do you think the odds against *that* were?"

"It *was* pretty lucky," Dave agreed, lifting his head off the pillow. "But it was *really* lucky not getting stuck on the Runnin' Rebels. Maybe we ought to give them a warning about Otto."

"Somehow I don't think we'll have to," Brian said. "Otto has a way of showing his true colors pretty quickly."

A shaft of moonlight shone through the cabin as the door was suddenly pushed open from the porch.

"Come on, you guys, quiet down in there." It was Big Lew again.

Brian forced himself to rest silently for a few minutes, but he was wide-awake.

"Yo, Dave," he whispered, trying not to be as loud as he'd been before. "What do you think of Slick?" Slick had taken a bunk on the other side of the cabin, and Brian was pretty sure he wouldn't overhear.

"Oh, you know, he's from Chicago. One of those know-it-all city dudes," Dave replied. "But no question, he can *play*! And when he does his Big Lew imitation, he's pretty funny."

"*Pretty* funny?" Brian retorted. "He cracks me up! He's kind of tough on Big Lew, though."

"Oh, I don't think he really means anything by it," Dave said. "He's a cool guy. Coolest guy *I've* seen here."

Brian thought quietly for a minute or two, running his hand over his fade haircut.

"I feel kind of bad for Will," he said to his friend. "Stuck on the Tar Heels with a bunch of strangers."

"Oh, you know Will," Dave replied. "He'll be running that team before you know it."

"Still . . . ," Brian said wistfully. "Hey, Dave, do you miss your own room at home?"

"Come on, Bri, we just left this morning!"

"You know what I mean."

"You mean, am I a little homesick?" Dave asked softly. "Yeah, I guess—"

Just then a beam from a flashlight flooded them both. Brian thought they'd been caught by Big Lew, but after his eyes adjusted to the sudden light, he saw that the flashlight was being wielded by Slick Washington from across the cabin.

"Aw, Lucius," Slick cooed, "looks like we got a couple of homesick pups over there. Lucius?" he continued in his lovey-dovey voice. "Do you miss yo' mama?"

"Hey, dude, at least I don't need to sleep with a night-light," Brian countered, nodding at Slick's flashlight.

"Whew," Slick laughed, turning on his Magic Johnson grin. "Trash talk from the Branford boy. Impressive!"

Heads popped up all over the cabin.

"Since everybody's wide-awake around here," Slick announced, "I thought I'd share a little top-secret information I picked up today. Judging from some scouting I did, we're going to kick some serious butt in Friday's tournament."

"How do you already know so much about who can do what around here?" Dave asked. "And how come Big Lew recognized you as soon as you got called over to the Wolverines?"

"I've been here before, my man!" Slick answered, his voice rising. "What do I look like, some kind of rookie?"

The conversation was interrupted by a loud, angry voice.

"All right! I've told you guys twice!" Big Lew yelled. "Next guy I hear mouthing off goes straight to Rock's office. Come on, gentlemen, you're in training. You need a good night's sleep." He shut the door again firmly. They heard his footsteps fade away out on the porch.

After a few minutes of silence, Brian wasn't at all surprised to hear a near-perfect imitation of Big Lew's high-pitched voice: "Come on, gentlemen, you're in training. You need a good night's sleep."

There was muffled laughter from all

over the cabin. Encouraged by the reaction, Slick went further. "Man, am I going to give that pasty-faced, girl-talking, wimpy excuse for a coach a week to remember!"

"Oh yeah?" Lucius challenged, obviously trying to egg his friend on. "What special treat you got up your sleeve this time?"

In answer, Slick stole out of his bunk and crept over to the door of the cabin. He opened it quietly and snuck out.

About five minutes later the door creaked open again. Brian saw a huge, wicked grin on Slick's face.

"What did you do?" Brian asked anxiously.

"Quiet!" Slick commanded. "Just watch a master at work."

Slick had gathered two handfuls of tiny pinecones that had fallen from the trees outside the cabin. Using his flashlight, he located Big Lew's stack of underwear in the counselor's cubby.

"Tighty whiteys," Slick said with scorn. "Figures the dork doesn't wear boxers." Brian watched as Slick carefully inserted one prickly pine cone inside each pair of Big Lew's briefs.

"That's *sick*!" Lucius crowed with admiration.

"Ouch!" Brian said, without really meaning to speak aloud. "Isn't that going to hurt him?"

Slick winked and smiled at him. "Only for a while. He'll get over it. In a few weeks."

Just what are we getting ourselves into? Brian wondered.

CHAPTER 4

"Hopwood. You seem to know what you're doing. Greg's guarding me. Here, you set a pick on him for me."

Will felt his face flush at being singled out by Jamie Townsend. Jamie was only five-nine—just five inches taller than Will himself. And though he didn't look the part of a big-time hoops star, with a scruffy, half-grown-in beard and a beat-up old baseball cap worn backward, he was one of the most popular counselors at camp. Will was pleased that he'd already made an impression on him.

Will stepped up alongside Greg, Jamie's

tall, quiet assistant counselor, so that they were almost shoulder to shoulder.

"Okay, Hopwood. How does this thing work?" Jamie asked, pretending to be learning along with the rest of the team.

"Well," Will said, "if you wanted to drive to your right, you'd run Greg right into me. Then you'd be free to take it to the hole."

"Sounds good. Let's give it a try." Jamie started dribbling to his right, but Greg was able to slide by Will and stay with Jamie.

"Hey, wait a minute," Jamie complained, as if he were really confused. "I thought I'm supposed to be free now. What went wrong here?"

One of the Tar Heels spoke up. "Will was standing *parallel* to Greg. That's why Greg was able to slide around him. If Will had been *perpendicular* to Greg, like this"—the boy set his chest almost up against the assistant's shoulder—"then Greg would have run into him, and Coach would have been free."

"Exactly!" Jamie said.

The Tar Heel doing the talking was known as MJ, an African American kid of medium height, a little on the skinny side. What really stood out about him, Will thought, were his clothes. He wore bright white wraparound sports goggles, an expensive purple and gold Laker warm-up suit, and the cleanest, newest high-tops on the team.

Will realized that MJ was right. What surprised him was that someone who looked as inexperienced as MJ knew the fine points of setting a pick. As a matter of fact, judging by what he'd seen in the first day and a half of camp, this kid seemed to know just about everything!

"Okay," Jamie said to the team. "You've earned a break. Take a few minutes. When you get back we'll start running a little half-court offense."

The practice was in the small gym, not the huge tournament arena. As he toweled off, Will glanced down at the opposite hoop, where Brian and Dave and the rest of the Wolverines were working out. When he'd run into his friends from home the first day and said it was no big deal that he wasn't on their team, he hadn't really meant it.

But now he was starting to like the Tar Heels. At least they didn't have any hot dogs, such as Slick Washington, Lucius Lanier, or, worst of all, Otto Meyerson.

"Everybody get some water?" Jamie asked as the boys returned to the floor. "All right, here we go. Hopwood, shirts. Shackleford, skins. Manning, shirts . . ."

Jamie divided the Tar Heels into two squads of four. He placed himself on skins and Greg on shirts to round out the teams.

Will was happy to find himself on the same team as MJ, Rex Manning, and Billy Lane. Rex was a tall, muscular kid with long red hair. His game needed some polish, but the talent was there. *He's a born power forward,* Will thought.

Billy was short, with straight dark hair. He seemed to dribble equally well with either hand—perfect point guard material.

"Okay, shirts," Jamie said, "you guys are going to be on offense for the first few possessions. I want to see you work the ball. Quick passes. Set picks for each other. Don't settle for the first shot you see."

As Jamie barked the instructions Will noticed all eyes were on the counselor. There was no nonsense, no horseplay. Down at the Wolverines' end of the gym, he heard a lot of goofing around. Mostly what he heard was Slick's laughter and Big Lew's high-pitched, irritated shouting.

Jamie blew his whistle, signaling the offense to start a play. Though Billy made a crisp entry pass to Will in the pivot, none of the other shirts seemed to be moving. But just as Will was about to be tied up by Lester Shackleford, he saw MJ sneak up alongside the tall skins center.

"Use it," MJ mouthed. Will moved quickly to his right, lost Shackleford on MJ's solid pick, and released a soft one-hander.

As they fell back to the mid-court line to set up again, Will pointed to MJ, as if to say, "I got the hoop, but this man should get the credit."

On the next play, Billy again worked the ball into Will in the paint, and Will immediately whipped it out to MJ in the left corner. But though MJ was wide open, he seemed reluctant to pull the trigger.

"Take it!" Will shouted.

Finally MJ let it fly.

Will had never seen such an awkward shot. MJ started by pushing the ball from down around his waist. His whole body lunged forward as he released it. He finished with his left leg lifted in the air and pointing backward, looking like an off-balance ballerina. *How can a guy who knows so much look that bad?* Will wondered.

But while Will was marveling at the ugliness of his shot, MJ flashed in for the rebound and instantly kicked the ball back out to Billy on the perimeter. Billy canned the fifteen-footer with no hesitation.

REBOUND!

"MJ, heads-up playing!" Jamie shouted. "And Billy, way to bury that open jumper!"

Will smiled. The counselor clearly liked what he saw.

Jamie let the shirts have the ball for two more possessions. On the first try, Billy penetrated to the hoop, then zipped a pass to Rex for a short corner jumper. *Good!* Will thought.

On the second possession, Billy put up a foul-line one-hander that was off, but MJ grabbed the rebound in front of Jamie on a picture-perfect box-out. Then he shoveled the ball back to Will, who connected on a ten-footer.

Will hadn't even had to call for the ball. MJ just knew he was there.

The shirts were starting to click.

These may not be the Bulls, Will thought, *but come the Monster Jam on Friday, this team could go somewhere.*

"All right," Jamie called, "you guys grab some water. Then we'll go with skins on offense."

As they waited in line at the cooler, Will asked MJ where he was from.

"Branford," MJ replied.

"Branford? Get outta here!" Will replied. "I'm from there, too. How come I've never seen you before?"

"Well," MJ explained, "my family's been living in L.A., and my parents wanted me to finish the school year there. So we just moved to Branford at the beginning of the summer. But I've already heard plenty about the Bulls."

Will straightened up proudly. Since he always considered himself the team leader, he took any insult or compliment to the Bulls personally.

There was another thing Will had been curious about. "What does *MJ* stand for?" he asked.

MJ frowned. "Michael Jordan."

Will laughed. "No, really," he said.

"Really." MJ sighed.

Will chuckled. He was laughing at the thought of a kid this uncoordinated having the name Michael Jordan. But MJ thought he was laughing because he didn't believe him.

"My name really is Michael Jordan," he said levelly. "You can check my birth certificate."

Just then Will heard the sarcastic voice of Lucius Lanier behind them. "Yeah, right," Lucius said, "and I'm Charles Barkley. You can check my driver's license." Lucius and Dave had come down to the Tar Heels' end of the court chasing after a loose ball.

Will felt his face get hot. "Butt out, Lanier," he said. "Why don't you just take your driver's license, drive back down to your end of the gym, and park yourself there!"

"Chill out, Will," Dave said. "You don't have to take everything so seriously. My man was just having a little fun."

Lucius was already gliding back to

the other basket as Dave spoke.

"Yeah," Will answered. "I guess nasty put-downs are what you and your new Wolverine buddies *would* call fun."

"Oh, come on, Will, give me a break," Dave said, glaring. "*You're* the one talking about new friends? I know you're Mr. Stand-Up-For-Your-Teammates, but get real. I mean, you just met this dude yesterday!"

With those words, Dave spun around and strode back toward the Wolverines.

Will was about to try to get in the last word when he heard Jamie call out, "Okay, Tar Heels—skins on offense, shirts on D."

Will put Dave out of his mind, and got ready to play defense.

5

"Free play!" Big Lew called out in his squeaky voice.

Slick no longer even had to *do* his Big Lew imitation. Now after one of the counselor's high-pitched announcements, all the Wolverines would just *look* at Slick and burst into laughter.

Big Lew had explained free play to them that morning. "You've got forty-five minutes between dinner and the evening activity, gentlemen," he'd said. "That is, unless you feel the need to pull a prank like the one you pulled last night." He had stopped his speech and glared at all the Wolverines.

Yes," he'd continued, "I found the pinecones in my underwear. And if you don't learn to respect private property, we'll all spend our free-play time sitting quietly in this cabin. If you can stay out of trouble, then you can use free play to read comic books, trade basketball cards, or write letters home. Or just in case you haven't had enough hoops during the day, you can shoot around some more."

He'd chuckled after his last comment, obviously thinking it was a funny idea. Brian noticed that Big Lew was the only one who laughed at his own jokes. *Actually,* Brian thought, *most of the kids do choose shooting around for free play. What's so funny about that? After all, this is basketball camp, isn't it?*

Slick grabbed a ball and jumped down the cabin's porch steps, followed by Lucius, Brian, and Dave. "You know, I was going to stay in and write letters tonight," Slick said. "I thought I'd write first to my own parents and then to Brian's and Dave's." He gave the two Branford boys his Magic-like grin. "You know, let them know how their homesick pups are doing."

Ever since Slick had overheard Brian confessing his homesickness the first night, it had been one of his running gags. But the kidding was good-natured, always accompanied by a wink and a grin. Though it didn't bother Brian at all, he was afraid the ribbing about their parents might upset Dave, whose dad had died of a sudden heart attack a few years ago. But the smile on Dave's face told him otherwise.

"How about it, Brian?" Slick continued to needle. "You feel homesick for that room of yours again tonight?"

"I feel like kicking your butt out on the court!" Brian countered. He'd discovered that the best way to handle Slick's constant wisecracking was to fire the trash talk right back at him.

They were heading for the Quad, four green asphalt courts stretched out between the two rows of cabins. The Quad courts were not superdeluxe, the way the one in the arena was. The asphalt had some cracks, and the rims sagged. But they were just fine for three-on-three pickup games, and that's what the four Wolverines were searching out.

Court Four was nearest their cabin. Brian noticed there were already two kids shooting around on it. One of them was tall and graceful, the other slightly shorter and remarkably awkward. Will and MJ, no doubt about it.

Lucius noticed them at the same time and started right in. "Well, if it isn't Will Hotshot and the real Michael Jordan, the one with the birth certificate to prove it."

"Lucius, be cool. This is free play," Slick said with his easy smile. "We're all here to have a good time."

For the first few minutes the six of them just shot around. Brian noticed that a good number of the shots were dropping in. Five of the players on the court were pretty decent. Only MJ, despite his high-priced Laker gear and his impressive knowledge of the game, didn't measure up.

Slick had a particularly hot hand. He had just made his way around the three-point circle, shooting six swishes in a row. "Okay, Slick's ready," he said. "Let's go three on three." He gestured at MJ. "C'mon, Hopwood, let's find a sixth who can actually play."

MJ looked into the distance, pretending he wasn't aware of the insult. Brian was stunned by Slick's meanness. Only two minutes earlier, Slick had acted as peacemaker when Lucius was mouthing off! *Man*, Brian thought, *who can figure this guy out*?

"We already have our six, Slick," Will said in a tone that left no room for argument. "I'll take MJ. Just pick who you want on your team."

"If you want to lose, dude, I don't care." Slick was all smiles again. "I'll take my man Lucius, of course, and I'll go with Dave the Rave. Brian, I'm afraid we're going to have to loan you to the Tar Heels. You said you felt like kicking my butt, anyway."

Brian stepped over to where Will and MJ were standing. After the heated words he'd exchanged with Will earlier in the day, he was kind of glad to be on their team. At the same time, he felt slighted that Slick had "traded" him.

"Your ball out," Dave offered.

"Okay, guys, let's go," Will called to his teammates.

Brian inbounded the ball to Will, who in turn passed it quickly to MJ. They kept the ball moving briskly, feeling out the defense for an opening.

"Man," Lucius complained, "I think we need a twenty-four-second clock for these dudes. You guys ever planning to shoot the ball, or what?"

At that point Lucius, who had been playing MJ loosely to begin with, backed off even further, daring the gawky player to shoot.

MJ glanced quickly at Will, who nodded. Then MJ launched one of his shot-putlike heaves. It thudded against the backboard and rebounded high off the front of the hoop. Then the ball rolled around the rim a few times—and fell in.

Slick dropped to the asphalt, feigning a heart attack. "You're going to count a brick like that?" he asked, looking first at MJ, then at Will.

"Last I heard," said Will calmly, "if it goes in, it counts. Just the same as a swish." He looked at Brian. "Or do you guys on the Wolverines play it differently?"

Brian could see what was brewing between Will and Slick, and he didn't want to get into it. "One-oh," he said simply. "We lead."

Lucius casually passed the ball in to Slick. Closely guarded by Will, Slick flipped it back out to Lucius. Dave kept cutting back and forth under the basket, waving to indicate that he was open. Brian, who was getting tired of chasing Dave, wondered why Lucius and Slick never looked for anyone but each other.

Lucius dribbled the ball way out in front of his body, unprotected, daring MJ to go for the steal. But MJ wouldn't bite. Finally Lucius lofted a one-hander over MJ's hands, from eighteen feet out. It was a high-arching shot that was right on target, snapping the net back on its way through.

"Splash!" Lucius said, admiring his own shot. **NOTHING BUT NET**

"Now *that's* what I call a basket," added Slick.

"One-one," Will said, ignoring their play-by-play.

Will tossed the ball in to Brian at the top of the key. Dave was guarding him tightly. Brian held the ball between his legs. He faked to the right, then dribbled into the left corner and put up a fadeaway jumper, his favorite shot. The release, the spin, everything felt perfect. But the shot was slightly off the mark.

Lucius pulled down the rebound and took it behind his back with a flourish. But MJ, anticipating the showboat move, stripped the ball and fired it out to Will, who was waiting at the foul line.

Will calmly made the fifteen-footer, then nodded and pointed his index finger at MJ. "Smart play," he said. "Two-one, ours."

The two teams went on trading baskets. Brian could tell by the no-nonsense look on Slick's face that the game was a lot tighter than he'd anticipated.

With Will's team up 9–8, Brian had the ball again at the top of the key. Again he made the fake to his right, but this time, just as he began his move to his left, Dave's hand flashed out to knock the ball loose. Lucius gained control of it and scored an easy layup.

"My bad," Brian said, apologizing for his turnover.

"Brian," Will said, "I think you might be overdoing that move. Maybe you ought to think about mixing it up a little. You know, try going right once in a while."

"Hey, Hopwood," Slick said. There was no smile on his face this time. "Who died and made you Master of the Moves?" Turning to Brian, he added, "You going to listen to some kiss up

44

who's always doing what the counselor tells him to do?"

Brian saw Will looking at him for support, but he found himself too annoyed by Will's "helpful" suggestion. "Will, I've got to tell you something," he said. "Whether we're back home in Branford or up here at Lake Winnetoba, one thing never changes. You're always trying to tell everyone how to play the game."

As soon as the words were out of his mouth, Brian wished he hadn't said them—but it was too late to take them back. He saw Will's face go bright red.

"Well, I guess nobody can tell you Wolverines anything," Will said flatly, trying to control his anger. "No wonder I hear your coach screaming at you all the time."

Slick grabbed the ball. "This game is getting tired fast," he said. "I'm outta here." Then Slick turned around and sauntered away from the Quad. Lucius followed him like a shadow.

Brian locked eyes with Will. "I'm right behind you," he said to Slick, turning to fall in line behind his Wolverine teammates. "You coming, Dave?"

Out of the corner of his eye, Brian saw Dave looking over at Will. Will shrugged as if to say, "Hey, your decision." Then Dave hurried to catch up to the rest of the Wolverines, leaving Will and MJ alone on the court.

6

"These canoes are so *cool*!" Brian crowed as he dipped his paddle into the lake. "Man, one stroke and this thing really takes off!"

"How about one stroke on the other side of the canoe for a change?" Slick suggested. He was lounging up front, with his feet dangling over the sides. "Then maybe we could actually get somewhere."

Brian, who'd been paddling only on the right side, gave Slick a sheepish grin. He was so excited just to be on the water that he hadn't realized they'd been going in circles!

Brian knew that Slick was letting him do all the paddling so he could just laze in the sun, but that was okay. Canoeing was something he'd never done before—and he was loving it.

"Hey, I just noticed," Brian said, looking at Slick. "You're not wearing a life jacket." Brian was wearing one of the orange vests all the campers had been told to put on before taking out a canoe.

"I wasn't planning to need one," Slick said coolly. "You know, Simmons," he continued, "you're starting to sound more like your buddy Hopwood all the time. I still might have to trade you to the Tar Heels."

"When did *you* get promoted to general manager?" Brian trash-talked back. "Did I miss something in the morning newspaper?"

The whoosh of an approaching canoe made Brian turn around. He recognized Lucius's neon-green tank top and Dave's ridiculous-looking sailor hat.

"Ahoy, mateys!" Dave called out, trying to sound like a pirate.

Lucius just rolled his eyes. "Hey, Slick, my man," he called over. "What do you think? Time for a PB and J sandwich?"

Brian could tell by Lucius's tone of voice that he wasn't talking about lunch. Brian turned to Slick with a puzzled look.

Slick was still sprawled back in the canoe, his hands locked together behind his head, forming a pillow. "A PB and J sandwich," he said with a mischievous grin, "is just what it sounds like. Two canoes kind of come together and smash another canoe between them." He took his hands from behind his head and clapped them together. The smack echoed across the lake.

Brian and Dave exchanged glances.

"Now, the way I see it," Slick continued, "you and me, Brian, we feel like bread. And Lucius and Dave over there," he said, winking at Dave, "I know *they* feel like bread. But you see that canoe way over on the other side of the lake?"

Brian shaded his eyes with his hands to screen out the sun and looked where Slick was pointing. He thought he could make out the figures of Will and MJ in a green canoe about a quarter of a mile across the water.

"Yeah, those guys," said Slick. "Hopwood and Jordan. To me, they look like peanut butter and jelly. You, Lucius?"

Lucius licked his lips. "Man, I can almost taste it," he said.

"Here's the story," Slick continued. "To tell you the truth, Hopwood's really been ticking me off. First he tells my man Lucius to get lost when we're all in the gym. Then he squeezes that MJ loser into our game yesterday. And *then* he has the nerve to tell my buddy Simmons which way he should make his move. You ask me, he's peanut butter."

"But that sounds dangerous," Brian objected. He was aware he sounded like a goody-goody, but he couldn't help it. "I don't think the lake is the place to screw around—"

"Simmons, what are you, a teacher's pet like your friend Hopwood?" taunted Slick. "Don't worry, we do it all the time. It'll just be a love tap."

Slick read the reluctance on Brian's face. "Come on, Brian," he said with his disarming grin. "It'll give you guys something to talk about when you're back home in Branford."

Before Brian had a chance to respond, he felt Slick propelling their canoe toward Will and MJ. Lucius and Dave were heading in the same direction, but at a slightly different angle.

"Hey, Captain, all paddled out?" Slick kidded. "I got to do all the work around here?"

Brian hesitantly dipped his paddle back in the water. *Maybe this isn't such a big deal,* he thought. *Just a little practical joke.* Besides, he was still somewhat annoyed at Will for that crack about overdoing his favorite move.

Since Brian was paddling halfheartedly, he was surprised that his canoe was closing in on Will's so rapidly. Then it dawned on him: Slick was paddling with all his strength! He looked to his right and saw Lucius and Dave also bearing down on the green canoe at full speed.

"Hey, what about that little love tap?" he asked Slick with alarm.

"Changed my mind, dude," Slick said, his eyes cold, his muscles straining. "Fasten your seat belt!"

Brian wanted desperately to do something, but he was helpless. "Will! MJ! Look out!" he yelled.

"Are you guys *demented*?" MJ screamed as he saw Slick and Brian careening toward him from one side and Lucius and Dave coming from the other.

The crunch of the impact, first one thud, then another, made Brian sick to his stomach. MJ somehow managed to keep his balance by grabbing the side of the canoe, but Will was flung overboard, landing back-first with a huge splash. Brian watched with horror as his friend went under.

He held his breath, expecting Will to

pop up any moment. But ten seconds went by and there was still no sign of him. Brian thought of jumping in. He thought of screaming for help. But he did nothing. He felt absolutely paralyzed.

Finally he saw Will's dark hair break the surface of the water alongside Lucius and Dave's canoe. Will was coughing and gulping for air, his life jacket keeping him afloat. Obviously he'd swallowed a lot of water.

"Got stuck under the canoe," Will gasped. "Didn't know which way was up." He was struggling to get the words out.

MJ was the only one with the presence of mind to reach out a paddle for Will to grab. Using all his strength, he helped his half-drowned partner climb back into the canoe.

"Just catch your breath first, Will," MJ said. "You don't need to explain what happened. It's *these* imbeciles," he sputtered angrily, glaring at the other four, "who should be doing the explaining. Do you all realize what could have *happened*?"

Slick rocked back on his seat, trying to

seem unshaken. "It's not that big a deal," he said quietly. "Just a little accident."

MJ was not about to be calmed down so fast. "Accident, my foot!" he shouted. "I might just *accidentally* report all of you to Rock's office!"

Brian was taking in none of this. All he could see in his head was the horrible sight of Will going under, and all he could hear was the echo of MJ screaming, "Do you all realize what could have *happened*?"

One of my best friends could have drowned, Brian thought, *and it would have been my fault. That's what could have happened!*

For the first time it occurred to Brian that maybe hanging out with Slick wasn't such a good idea. Yet something told him it was important to stay on Slick's good side. He remembered the way Slick had cruelly humiliated MJ the night before at the Quad.

MJ, Brian could see, was not on Slick's good side. And, obviously, neither was Will.

7

Shawn Kemp slam-dunked over Cliff Robinson as Will watched in amazement. He could almost feel their sweat flying in his face.

Will had heard about Wednesday Night Hoopla—next to the Monster Jam, it was the most talked-about event at camp. It took place in the Coliseum, an open-air, horseshoe-shaped structure with stadium-style seating. At the closed end was the stage, with a large screen, and in the middle of the interior grassy area was a bonfire pit.

Will was used to viewing NBA highlights

every morning on ESPN, but he'd never seen them on a screen that measured twenty-one feet by fourteen feet before. Talk about in-your-face hoops!

And with the flames from the bonfire leaping almost twenty feet high in front of the humongous screen, there was only one word for the whole experience: *awesome*!

Rock had kicked off the evening with stories of his short NBA career. "You've all heard of the Big O, Oscar Robertson? Well, Milwaukee drafted me to be his backcourt partner. If my back hadn't gone out on me, history might still be talking about Big O and the Rock. . . ."

Rock seemed a lot more upbeat onstage than he did booming out announcements during the day. Will figured he was really a nice guy who just tried to *seem* scary so he'd be able to keep up the discipline around camp.

The big-screen highlights were followed by a sing-along, and then everybody roasted marshmallows. It was during the marshmallow roast that MJ managed to steer Will into a conversation about the Branford Bulls.

"Derek and Jo are definitely awesome," MJ offered, "and Mark's pretty decent. But how did Chunky Schwartz ever make the team?"

"Hey, for a new kid in town, you sure know what's happening with the Bulls," Will observed.

"Of course I do! Who in Branford doesn't?"

Will swelled up. He loved this kind of admiration. It was part of what being a Bull was all about.

"You see what I was thinking," MJ pushed on hesitantly, "is that I'm probably almost as good as Chunky. And now that we're, you know, sort of friends, I thought maybe I could get a shot at the Bulls. I mean, like, just as a role player. . . ."

Will finally realized why MJ had turned the subject in this direction. "MJ, don't keep putting yourself down! With your smarts, you do a lot of good things out there. Of course the Bulls can give you a look when we get back home."

MJ's expression brightened a little at Will's support but then darkened again quickly. "I guess I haven't exactly helped my chances by making enemies of Brian and Dave," he said glumly.

"Don't worry. *I'm* the one who makes the decisions on the Bulls," Will boasted. He was glad Brian and Dave weren't there to contradict him. Suddenly he felt a knot in his stomach. The mention of Brian and Dave had taken the edge off his excitement about Wednesday Night Hoopla.

"You know," he confided to MJ, "I don't know what's up with those two. That business at the Quad the other night, and then that canoe stunt yesterday . . ." He stretched out his long arms and thought for a while. "It's got to have something to do with Slick Washington. He seems like really bad news to me."

"Yeah, Slick and Lucius, Dumb and Dumber," MJ said. "And don't forget their good pal Otto Meyerson."

Will looked confused. "What do you mean, their good pal?"

MJ nodded at a group of kids across the Coliseum from where they were sitting. Will followed his glance and saw Slick, Lucius, and Otto clowning around.

"From what I hear, Slick and Otto are like this," MJ replied, crossing his fingers. "They were both in the same bunk last year. I heard they got into so much trouble that Rock made sure they weren't together again this year."

"Well, well," Will muttered thoughtfully. "Slick and Otto are good buds." He added sarcastically, "Now who would have ever thought *they* had anything in common?"

Brian was thankful that the road from the Coliseum back to the cabins was downhill. Between basketball, the canoeing adventure, and Wednesday Night Hoopla, it had been quite a day. He was exhausted.

"Bet I'll be snoring before Big Lew even calls lights out tonight," he said to Dave.

"Yeah," Dave said. "That's if Slick and Lucius can manage to keep their mouths shut for once. Those two never seem to get tired of screwing around. I don't know how—"

Suddenly Brian shoved a hand in front of Dave's mouth. He silently pointed out two figures just off to the side of the road. The voices sounded familiar. And the name *Hopwood* came up over and over again.

Brian quietly moved behind a tall evergreen, gesturing for Dave to follow, so they could hear more without being seen.

"All we gotta do," one voice said, "is throw elbows, grab on to their jerseys, trip them. You know, that kind of stuff. Shove them around a little."

"That's Slick talking!" Dave cried hoarsely.

"I know. Shhh," Brian whispered.

"Cheap shots, you mean," Lucius said. "Like when the ref's not looking?"

"You got it, dude," Slick said. "We keep that up for a while, and even Boy Scouts like Hopwood and Jordan'll take a swing at somebody. Ref sees that, and Hopwood's gone. History. Serve that coach's pet right!"

"They're trying to get Will thrown out of the Monster Jam," Dave said angrily, attempting not so successfully to whisper. "Man, we ought to go punch their lights out—"

"Keep it down!" Brian hissed. "What are you, mental? Let's hear the whole deal before you go into your hero act."

"Hey, why don't we get Meyerson to help out?" Lucius suggested. "He's the best cheap-shot artist around."

"You can say that again," Brian couldn't resist whispering to Dave.

"Now here's the best part," Slick bragged. "We'll even get Beavis and Butt-head in on it."

Brian and Dave looked at each other. Brian felt as though someone had just punched him in the stomach. He had a pretty good idea of who Slick meant by Beavis and Butt-head.

"If I jumped off the Empire State Building," Slick continued, "those two followers would be right behind me. What a pair of losers! Come on, let's go find Meyerson."

Brian and Dave were speechless. Brian felt his face get hot with anger and shame. So that was the kind of leader they'd been following!

What made Brian most ashamed was that he recognized a lot of truth in what Slick said. When Slick had told them to jump, he and Dave had jumped.

Dave, who was never very good at keeping quiet for long, was the first to speak. "Dude, we gotta tell Will right away," he said with determination.

But Brian, despite his rage, was thinking more clearly. "No," he said with quiet fury. "That would let that two-faced Slick off the hook too easily. Will would just tell him off, or maybe they'd get into a fight, and that would be that." He thought some more. "No, we've got to play along. Wait for things to unfold a little."

Dave looked at him, not comprehending.

"Dave," Brian said, "we're going to make that double-crosser sorry he ever messed with Beavis and Butt-head. I'm not sure exactly how, but I swear to you, one way or another we'll get this plot to backfire on Slick Washington. Come on, let's follow them to our old pal Meyerson!"

Brian and Dave stayed about fifty yards behind Slick and Lucius, constantly weaving between trees to stay out of sight.

They waited quietly until Slick and Lucius had entered the Runnin' Rebels cabin. Then Brian ducked under the porch. Dave followed, tripping again, this time over a raised tree root.

"What are we doing under here?" Dave whispered, nursing a scraped knee. "This place gives me the creeps. And how are we going to see what those two are doing?"

"No problem," Brian whispered back. "We won't have to see a thing. With those two loudmouths, hearing will be just fine."

Brian was right. "Yo, guys, where's

Otto?" he heard Slick ask, from directly overhead.

"Where do you think?" answered one of the Runnin' Rebels. "He's in Rock's office, as usual. Got caught mooning some little kids on the way back from Wednesday Night Hoopla. What an idiot!"

"Sounds like they know our boy Otto, all right," Dave whispered to Brian.

"Listen," Slick said, "me and Lucius have a little business to discuss with Otto. But since he's not here, I'm going to leave a note on his bunk. This is a private matter, so don't let me hear about anybody getting nosy."

The boys from Branford heard Slick and Lucius pounding down the porch steps, then saw them heading off in the direction of the Wolverines' cabin. When the coast was clear, Brian spelled out a plan to Dave. Dave kept nodding.

After a few minutes Dave popped out from under the porch where they'd been hiding and quickly ran into the cabin. "Hey, guys," Brian heard him shout. "You've got to see this! Two skunks fighting out behind the bunk. It's awesome!"

The Runnin' Rebels poured out the door, following Dave. As the cabin cleared out, Brian slipped in the front door and quickly tried to locate Otto's bunk.

"Guess they're gone," Brian heard Dave say outside. "I swear they were here a minute ago."

"Sure they were," said a tough-sounding kid who Brian figured must be the leader. "Hey, man, do me a favor. Next time if you think you see Santa Claus up on the roof, don't bother telling us about it."

The Runnin' Rebels would be back any second. Brian had to act fast. Out of the corner of his eye he caught a glimpse of a piece of white paper tucked under a pillow. He ran to snatch it.

The Runnin' Rebels laughed as they headed back to the front of the cabin. Brian met them on the porch steps.

"What were you doing in there?" the leader asked suspiciously.

"Just looking for Otto. Guess he's not around," Brian answered, trying to sound natural.

"All of a sudden that jerk Otto's Mr. Popularity," the tough kid said. "Go figure."

As the Runnin' Rebels filed back into their cabin, Brian and Dave walked away quickly. "Got it?" Dave asked anxiously.

Brian broke into a wide smile. "Got it," he said.

Brian felt a cool morning breeze as he and Dave walked to Rock's office, but he was sweating anyway. All they had to do was talk their way into using the photocopier to make a duplicate of Slick's note! Why was he so sure whoever was in the office would know what they were really planning?

"Hi, guys, what's happening?" Marsha, Rock's assistant, greeted the boys as they entered the office. She was so pretty the boys in camp almost didn't mind getting sent to the office. Except that it also meant having to deal with Rock.

"Oh, we're just copying some plays for Big Lew," said Dave, almost too quickly. "You know, getting ready for the Monster Jam," he added, trying to sound more natural.

Marsha shook her long black hair and laughed. "That Big Lew is a character," she said. "You'd think he was coaching for the NBA championship!" She smiled at the boys. "Go right ahead."

Brian photocopied the note. He was removing the original from the top of the copy machine when he heard a deep voice asking, "What are you boys up to?"

It was Rock, his shaved head towering over them as he stood in the doorway to the office.

"Just making some copies for Big Lew," Brian mumbled.

"Well, finish up and head back to your bunk for cleanup," Rock boomed. The surprising pleasantness that had been in his voice during Wednesday Night Hoopla was gone. He was back to his old, scary self.

As soon as Rock had left, the boys

thanked Marsha and quickly headed for the Runnin' Rebels' cabin.

When they arrived, Brian peeked in the window. Perfect timing! Cleanup was over, and the Rebels had already gone off to their first activity. Brian stuck the original of Slick's note under Otto's pillow, just where he had found it the night before. Then he tapped Dave on the shoulder and they made a mad dash for their own bunk.

Brian and Dave didn't slow down until they reached the porch of their own cabin. They were both out of breath.

"Whew!" Dave said. "That was the hard part. Now all we've got to do is get the copy to Big Lew and let him catch those suckers in the act." He paused, and his blue eyes clouded in a look of doubt. "Hey, Brian? You sure Big Lew's going to want to blow the whistle on two of his superstars with the Monster Jam on the line?"

"Yeah, I thought about that," Brian answered. "But Big Lew likes to do everything by the book. I think he'd blow the whistle on his own *mother* if she screwed up."

"You're probably right," Dave agreed. "But how are we going to get the copy of Slick's note into Big Lew's hands without coming off like the tattletales of the century?" he asked.

Brian's jaw tightened in concentration. He was confident he could figure this one out. Maybe he wasn't the world's greatest student, but he was a pro at this kind of thinking!

In a few seconds the perfect idea popped into his head. "I've got it!" Brian said. "You know Laura, Big Lew's girlfriend?"

"Yeah, but she's not here at camp," Dave pointed out.

Brian rolled his eyes. "No duh! *Of course* she's not here at camp. I'm talking about her *picture*."

"You mean the one on the shelf over his bed? The one that the big turkey kisses every night before he starts snoring?"

"Exactly," Brian said. "Now, if we attach the note to that photo—"

Dave finished the sentence for him: "Then Big Lew'll be sure to see it. And ol' Slick will get what's coming to him."

"Exactly!" said Brian again, triumphantly. But as he was enjoying the brilliance of his solution, he saw a frantic expression steal over Dave's face. Brian turned around.

There stood Slick Washington.

Brian's heart sank.

Slick broke the awkward silence. "Am I interrupting something?" he asked with his trademark grin.

"Nothing important," Brian said, and laughed nervously.

"Yo, dudes," Slick went on. Brian was grateful that Slick seemed to have something else on his mind. Maybe he hadn't heard what they were talking about. "I've got a plan for your buddies Will and MJ," Slick continued, "just a little friendly payback." He began to outline his scheme.

Brian and Dave did a good job of listening, pretending to be hearing the idea for the first time. Brian noticed that Slick left out any mention of getting Will and MJ thrown out of the tournament. He felt his blood boil, but he let Slick keep talking.

"What about it, guys?" Slick asked. "You're my good buddies. Can I count you in?"

"Yeah," Brian said finally to Slick, as if he'd had to think it over really carefully. "I guess you can count us in."

CHAPTER 9

Normally Brian would have been thrilled by all the fanfare. Rows of multicolored banners extended down from the roof of the arena. The overhead electronic scoreboard was lit up and ready to go. And the two teams were being introduced over the PA system.

This was the Monster Jam. This was what they'd all been waiting for since the first day of camp.

The format was a killer. Sixteen teams started the day in a single-elimination setup. The games of the first two rounds would be played on various courts throughout the camp, but the semifinals and the finals would take place in the Arena.

Brian knew it would take four wins—128 minutes of full-court basketball—for a team to survive as the All-Star Hoops Camp champions.

And here were his Wolverines in the semifinals, in front of bleachers packed to the top row with campers whose teams had already been knocked out. He saw the gold jerseys of the Bruins, the gray of the Hoyas, the red of the Hoosiers. Half were screaming for the Wolverines, half for their opponent, the Blue Devils.

On any other day Brian would have loved this kind of pressure. But that day there was too much on his mind.

He felt incredibly guilty over the way he'd turned his back on Will during the week. He was furious at Slick for pulling the wool over his eyes by acting as though they were good buddies, and he was mad at himself for falling for it.

Just a few minutes earlier, he and

Dave had watched as Otto elbowed, shoved, and tripped Will in the other semifinal matchup. The Tar Heels had trounced the Runnin' Rebels, but Otto had gotten away with murder, almost ripping Will's arms from their sockets.

Brian had been sorely tempted to spill the beans to Will right then and there. *Did Big Lew ever get that note?* he'd found himself wondering. *And is he going to do anything about it?*

Now Brian and Will had traded places. Will, whose Tar Heels had breezed through the tournament, was watching the Wolverines play the Blue Devils, to see who his team would meet in the finals. Brian could feel Will's eyes on him as he released a jumper from the left side.

Another brick off the back iron! Brian had never suffered through a game like this in his life. He knew if he could just can a shot or two, he'd get back his rhythm, but so far he couldn't buy a basket. With a little over a minute left in the half, he had a whopping zero points!

Brian had noticed that so far that day Slick and Lucius were hogging the ball even more than they normally did. Had they figured out that he and Dave were on to their plan? The Wolverines had muddled through with sloppy victories over the Hoyas and the Bruins, but they'd gotten by on natural talent. No teamwork at all.

With all this going through his mind, it was no wonder he couldn't hit a shot! He could just hear Jim and Nate, the Branford Bulls' coaches, telling the team that focus was the most important thing during a game. Focus, that was a laugh! In the first half against the Blue Devils, he was about as unfocused as a player could get!

He watched from his forward position as Dave dribbled the ball up the floor and threw a pass into the right corner—straight into the bleachers!

"What was that?" Slick screamed at Dave in frustration, throwing up his hands.

"That was to you," Dave said. "You should have been cutting!"

"Should have been," Slick mocked, shaking his head. "How about passing to where I *am* instead of where I *should have been*?"

On the Wolverines' next possession, Dave pushed the ball up the floor in a hurry. They were falling further and further behind, and Brian could tell Dave was trying to make something happen. He found Brian in his favorite spot along the left baseline and slid him a hard bounce pass.

As Brian squared up, he heard Slick call for the ball in the pivot. *Why should I pass the ball to him?* Brian asked himself. *I'll never see it again if I do.* On top of that, Brian was desperate to make a shot.

Up he went, but he had thought too much about it. The shot fell way short.

"Simmons, you trying to set a record or something?" Slick yelled in disgust. "That's about ten in a row!"

With Slick jawing at Brian, Brian's man scored an easy hoop at the other end. Brian had never even gotten back on defense.

"Come on, Brian," Dave called out. "Put it out of your mind. You'll score the next time down."

But Lucius grabbed the ball after the Blue Devils' basket and inbounded to Slick. Slick went coast to coast and swooped in for a layup.

Brian did manage to squeeze off one more shot before halftime, but this one banged off the backboard with a thud. Not even close.

"Yo, dude!" yelled Slick as the buzzer sounded with the Wolverines down 29–12. "Enough bricks for the day. Second half, you just keep dishing it to

Slick. Let me take care of the rest."

Brian headed for the men's room instead of the Wolverines' bench, a towel over his head, staring down at his black hightops. He didn't want to see Slick. He didn't want to see Big Lew. He didn't want to see anybody.

But a familiar voice broke through to him.

"Hey, Brian, what's happening to show time?"

It was Will, about the last person on earth he wanted to run into right then.

"And who's Slick Washington to tell Brian Simmons to stop shooting?" Will continued.

This caught Brian totally by surprise. Obviously Will had heard Slick's comment to Brian at the halftime buzzer. And obviously Will was still on Brian's side.

"You going to listen to that clown?" Will went on. "Bri, I'm surprised at you. You know real shooters never stop shooting. C'mon, keep putting them up. They'll start to fall." Will gave

Brian a punch on the arm, then headed back out to the bleachers.

Brian couldn't even speak. He had expected taunts about his horrendous shooting, or accusations about the canoe incident, or insults as payback for his outburst at the Quad, or anger for calling Will a "teacher" that first day by the cafeteria. No. Just "C'mon, keep putting them up. They'll start to fall."

He wandered over to the Wolverines' bench. There was a lot of shouting going on.

Big Lew was shouting about sharing the ball, about heart, about comebacks he had seen over the years.

Dave was shouting about two-man teams who never looked for anyone else.

Slick was shouting about gunners who kept firing even after missing every shot they'd taken.

Brian heard none of it. All he could hear was, *Keep putting them up. They'll start to fall.*

The Wolverines and the Blue Devils took the floor for the second half. Brian blotted out the screaming crowd in the overflowing bleachers. He blotted out the electronic scoreboard, which showed his team down by seventeen. He blotted out the scheming of Slick and Lucius and his own dismal first-half performance.

Keep putting them up. They'll start to fall.

On the first trip up the floor for the Wolverines, Dave passed Brian the ball on the left side. Brian dribbled into the corner and rose up smoothly for his fadeaway jumper. He didn't really have to look at the basket to know the result. Perfect release. Perfect rotation.

Brian was on the board.

"Way to hit it, Simmons!" he heard Big Lew cheer.

"Show time!" Will shouted.

Spurred on by the quick bucket, the Wolverines' defense picked up in intensity, too. The Blue Devils, who had scored effortlessly in the first half, had trouble even getting off a shot.

Brian drained three jumpers in the first minute and a half. His shots never even touched the rim. The Blue Devils' lead was down to eleven. All of a sudden there seemed to be a ball game again.

Brian noticed that Slick had stopped mouthing off at him and constantly calling for the ball. *He's probably not happy about not being the main man,* Brian thought, *but at least he knows a hot hand when he sees one.*

After Brian sliced through the lane for his fourth straight bucket, moving the Wolverines to within nine points, the Blue Devils called a time-out. But Brian knew it wouldn't cool him off. He had his focus back. He could feel it.

After the break, Brian found himself double-teamed as soon as he got his hands on the ball. Instinctively he kicked it back out to Dave at the top of the circle, and Dave lofted up a beauty. Bingo!

TWO POINTS!

Brian's confidence was contagious. All of the Wolverines started hitting their shots. The side of the arena pulling for the Wolverines went crazy. The other half of the gym groaned and fidgeted.

The final score was Wolverines 50, Blue Devils 46. Brian had remained red-hot, scoring twenty-one points in the second half. The Wolverines were now headed for a final-round meeting with the Tar Heels.

Brian could hardly contain himself as his team yelled, "Two, four, six, eight . . ." As soon as the cheer was finished, he rushed over to find Will, who met him with a low five.

"I told you to keep shooting," Will said with a smile, "but I didn't tell you to set the place on fire!"

"Will," Brian said, looking up at him sheepishly, "I don't know how you can even talk to me after how obnoxious I've been all week—"

"Have you been more obnoxious than usual?" Will asked with a straight face. "I hadn't noticed."

Clearly Will had made the decision to let him off the hook easily. That made Brian feel even worse.

"There's something else I've got to tell you," he blurted out.

It didn't matter that he and Dave had planned to keep Slick's plot a secret so that Slick would be caught in the act. There on the sidelines with Will, he just couldn't hold it in anymore. It all came pouring out: the overheard conversation following Wednesday Night Hoopla, the stolen note, and the copy for Big Lew attached to the photo of his girlfriend.

Brian watched as Will absorbed the information. "So that's why I took such a beating from Meyerson in the semis," Will said finally. "And I thought it was just the usual Branford-Sampton rough stuff."

After a long pause, Will added, "You know, I thought Washington was a jerk right from the beginning. But this plan to get me kicked out of the tournament? Man, that's low even for him."

Will's on-target reading of the Wolverines' ringleader made Brian feel even guiltier for following Slick. He didn't think he could stand waiting anymore. "Why don't we just go up to Big Lew and Rock, tell them exactly what we know, and let them nail Slick right now?"

"Whoa, Bri," Will said, holding up his hands. "Slow down. So far, what are they going to nail him for? For having a conversation with Lucius? For writing a note to Otto? No, you had it right the first time. Let it play out. Let Big Lew and Rock catch Slick in the act."

"But Will," Brian said with concern, "Slick and Lucius really have it in for you. They might take your head off!"

Will shrugged. "A few more cheap shots? No big deal." Slowly a big smile spread over his face. "It'll be worth the pain to see Slick Washington thumbed out of the Monster Jam!"

CHAPTER 10

By three o'clock, less than one hour after the Wolverines had polished off the Blue Devils, they took the floor for the fourth time—for the finals of the Monster Jam tournament. Now Brian knew what the guys in the NBA must feel like when they played three road games in four nights!

The bleachers had been packed for the semifinals. Now, with the blue-and-white shirted Blue Devils joining the spectators, there wasn't a space left in the stands.

"Come on, Tar Heels!"

"Go get 'em, Wolverines!"

Brian had to chuckle at the sound of all the shouting. *If only they knew what was really going on,* he thought. So much more than just a basketball game! With all the schemes and counterschemes, he could hardly keep track of who knew what.

As the players shook hands before the jump ball, Brian saw Slick give him a quick wink. *Yeah, you can count us in,* Brian thought. *In your dreams!*

The Wolverines scored first on a pretty play off the tip. Slick back-tapped it to Dave, who heaved it up-court to Lucius, racing for the hoop. Easy layup.

But the Tar Heels came right back on a nice feed from Billy Lane to Will, catching Slick out of position.

Up and back. Up and back. Trading baskets. The Wolverines had more talent, but the Tar Heels made up for it with their excellent teamwork.

"Watch the picks! Keep up the pressure!" Brian could hear Big Lew's high-pitched squeals from the Wolverines' bench. And the screaming from the bleachers, half for the Wolverines and half for the Tar Heels, was getting louder with each basket.

But Brian was having trouble concentrating on the game itself. He was waiting for the first cheap shot. He didn't have to wait long.

Barely two minutes into the game, Lucius threw a shoulder into Will, who was guarding Slick. It jolted Will out of the play.

"Number eleven, gold," the ref shouted, swooping down at Lucius and pointing to the back of his jersey. "Illegal pick! Blue ball."

Lucius had a puzzled look on his face. Brian knew this was just the kind of move he expected the referee not to notice. *Guess Big Lew got the message and tipped off the refs,* he thought with satisfaction.

Just a few plays later, MJ went up for a rebound. Slick ducked under him, causing him to land on his back. Slick grabbed the ball, but as he cradled it the whistle blew.

"Number thirty-two, gold," the ref yelled, pointing at Slick. "Loose-ball foul!"

Brian saw the same baffled look on Slick's face that he had seen on Lucius's a moment earlier. Dave ran over to Brian. "This is too sweet," he said in a hoarse whisper, so that only Brian could hear. "Slick and Lucius are used to pulling this stuff while the refs are looking the other way. Except now the zebras are watching every move they make. I love it!"

On the Tar Heels' next possession, Slick was called for a hand-check as he grabbed Will's jersey. He glared at Brian.

Brian understood the look. It meant,

Why are Lucius and I doing all the dirty work? What happened to you and Dave being in on this with us?

The Tar Heels hit a hot streak just before the end of the first quarter. Will canned a turnaround jumper from close range, and Billy Lane, their point guard, drained two one-handers from just inside the three-point circle. The six-point run put the Tar Heels up 14–10 and forced Big Lew to call a time-out.

Big Lew wanted the Wolverines to come out of their zone defense and play the Tar Heels man-to-man. Slick, barely listening, grumbled, "It might help if everyone did what they were supposed to."

"Hey, everybody's working hard," Big Lew said. "What are you talking about?"

Slick looked at Brian and Dave sullenly. "They know what I mean."

The second quarter started out looking like a video replay of the first: The two teams traded baskets, neither getting the upper hand. The Tar Heel guards went cold, but Will and Rex Manning, the power forward, picked up the scoring from the inside. For the Wolverines, Slick and Lucius continued to put most of the points on the board. In fact, the ball was hardly ever out of their hands.

With three minutes and forty seconds left in the period, Will muscled in to score on a put-back of Lester Shackleford's miss. As he hustled to get back on defense, he was knocked off balance by an intentional elbow thrown by Lucius. The ref hit Lucius with a technical and gave him a warning.

"What are you guys, refs or the police?" Lucius muttered.

For a while it appeared the half would end without further incident. But then it happened.

There were just thirty-two seconds left on the clock, with the Tar Heels up 24–21. Will had Slick beaten with a strong move to his right when Slick suddenly stuck his left leg out and tripped him. Will toppled to the hardwood floor with a crash, the ball skipping out of bounds.

The ref rushed at Slick. "Flagrant foul, number thirty-two." Pointing to the bleachers, he added, "You're out of the game!"

"Out of the game?" Slick said with a cool smile, as if he still had everything under control. "What about my warning?"

Big Lew bounced off the bench, furious. "You've had plenty of warnings, right from the first day of camp. And I'll tell you something else, Washington. You thought I was an easy mark, but you picked the wrong guy to mess with!"

"Big talk from Big Lew," Slick returned, smirking. "How you planning on winning without me?"

"I'd rather lose without you than win with you," Big Lew said angrily.

"I'd rather lose without you than win with you," Slick said, mimicking Big Lew's high voice and looking at his Wolverine teammates.

This time none of them laughed.

As Slick and Big Lew continued to shout at each other, Brian saw Rock slowly rising from his seat at the scorer's table. He had a sheet of paper in his hand. Brian could see that it was the du-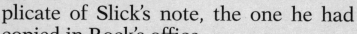plicate of Slick's note, the one he had copied in Rock's office.

Slick caught sight of Rock approaching. He too saw the sheet. The smirk suddenly vanished from his face.

"One more thing . . . ," Rock boomed.

Not a soul was even whispering in the stands. Everyone was waiting to hear what Rock had to say.

Rock held the note out in front of Slick, so it was perfectly clear what he was talking about.

"You're not only out of the game, Washington. You and your buddies Lanier and Meyerson are out of this camp. And you're never coming back.

Go on, pack your bags."

The campers in the bleachers watched in stunned silence.

Slick tried to keep his cool as he shuffled off the court. He glared at Brian and Dave.

Guess he put two and two together, Brian thought.

"Thought you dudes were cool," Slick muttered at them accusingly. No grin this time. No wink.

"No, we thought *you* were cool," Brian answered, looking him right in the eye. "But now everyone knows what you're really all about."

As Slick sauntered to the door, Brian called after him, "Oh, and Slick, enjoy that jump off the Empire State Building. Beavis and Butt-head would love to follow you, but we've got a game to finish."

Slick shot him one last dirty look, then slunk out of the arena.

After the refs and counselors settled everyone down, the game resumed. But the crowd continued to buzz. Hardly anyone was following the contest itself.

Brian was surprised at his own reaction. He felt relaxed for the first time in days. Sure, with Slick and Lucius gone, it would be a huge challenge to beat the Tar Heels. But at least with all the scheming out of the way, he could concentrate on playing basketball.

Brian and Dave and their teammates gave it their best shot. But their opponents were just too tough. An unusually strong team to begin with, now the Tar Heels were playing with sky-high confidence. Without Slick and Lucius, the Wolverines were simply out-manned.

The final score was Tar Heels 49, Wolverines 37.

CHAPTER 11

"I've got the last row!" Dave called as he scrambled to the back of the bus.

"Dave, you're such a baby," Brian said—and then tried to dash past Dave to get to the back first.

"What's the big deal about the last row?" MJ asked.

"If you're in the last row, you can make faces at the cars behind us," Will explained in his superior tone. "As you can see, your new friends from Branford are *very* mature."

"Oh, and I guess this kind of horseplay is beneath Mr. Most Valuable Player," said Dave.

At the closing ceremonies following the Wolverines–Tar Heels final, Will had come away with the MVP award for the whole All-Star Hoops Camp. And MJ had been named Most Improved Player.

After facing the Tar Heels in the finals, Brian had to agree with both selections.

"You superstars think you'll be needing any help carrying all your loot home from the bus?" Brian kidded.

Will and MJ had in fact made quite a haul. They had their MVP and Most Improved Player trophies, their huge championship team trophies, and their Monster Jam championship T-shirts. All this in *addition* to the small trophies presented to all the campers.

Will pretended not to hear the needling and spoke directly to MJ. "Remember, no game this weekend, but be at practice Monday, four o'-clock, at Jefferson."

Brian raised an eyebrow, and he saw that Dave had a similar expression on his face. Will explained that he'd promised MJ a shot with the Bulls. He didn't think anyone would mind.

"Sure, that's cool," Brian agreed after a moment's pause.

But he saw that Dave still had a concerned look on his face. He'd seen the look before. Though Dave was one of the best ball handlers in the league, he still got nervous every time the Bulls thought about taking on a new player.

"Don't sweat it, Dave," Will laughed. "MJ won't be stealing your job. I'm sure you've noticed that he's not exactly point guard material. But MJ's a real smart player, and he'll give us some more bench strength."

Dave seemed satisfied with the explanation. "You know, it feels funny to be talking about the Bulls again," Dave said. "I mean, we've been Wolverines and Tar Heels all week. I don't even remember who we have coming up on the schedule."

"This week's our bye week," Will jumped in. He never forgot anything about the Bulls. "Then we have Winsted, then Torrington, and then—"

"The Sampton Slashers!" Brian and Dave sang out together. That was one game none of them could forget.

"I gotta say," Dave said, "I don't think we've ever been in better shape to face those guys. You know, I hate to admit it, but we actually learned some good stuff from that crazy Big Lew."

"And with MJ joining our team," Will added, "we'll be three deep on the bench. We've never had that luxury before."

"And don't forget the intangibles," Brian said, using a word that Jim and Nate, their coaches, liked to use.

"Such as?" asked Dave.

Everyone looked at Brian.

"Well," he started slowly, "we don't have anyone on the team called Slick or Lucius. Or Otto."

"Don't even mention their names!" Will said.

"And we never have to play four games in one day," Brian added.

"That was too much!" MJ agreed.

"And after all we've been through this week," Brian concluded, smiling at Dave and MJ and Will, "I guess you could say we really know who our friends are."

About the Author

Hank Herman is a writer and newspaper columnist who lives in Connecticut with his wife, Carol, and their three sons, Matt, Greg, and Robby.

His column, The Home Team, appears in the *Westport News*. It's about kids, sports, and life in the suburbs.

Although Mr. Herman was formerly the editor-in-chief of *Health* magazine, he now writes mostly about sports. At one time, he was a tennis teacher, and he has also run the New York City Marathon. He coaches kids' basketball every winter and Little League baseball every spring.

He runs, bicycles, skis, kayaks, and plays tennis and basketball on a regular basis. Mr. Herman admits that he probably spends about as much time playing, coaching, and following sports as he does writing.

Of all sports, basketball is his favorite.

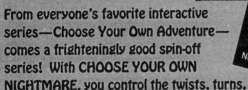